CONSIDER THE POSSIBILITIES

STEPHAN JAMES

Published by Water Dragon Publishing
waterdragonpublishing.com

ISBN 978-1-962538-45-9 (Trade Paperback)

FIRST EDITION

10 9 8 7 6 5 4 3 2 1

AUTHOR'S NOTE

This story began, as many do, with a writing practice session and expanded from there. There is a lot of conversation these days about multiverses and quantum entanglement, and most of it seems very far removed. While the surface of this story si about those concepts, turns out it's actually about the personal and societal changes that we've all experienced over the past few decades. And whether or not we are prepared to deal with those that are to come in the future.

CONSIDER THE POSSIBILITIES

I F HE'D SEEN ME FIRST, he might have shied away from knocking on my door before 8 am on a Saturday. I can't imagine what I looked like after four hours of sleep in the past two nights, unshaven, bleary-eyed and worn down from worry and beating myself up. But he had no visibility from the porch, obviously, which is why he felt the liberty to assault the door frame.

Bang, bang, bang came the noise, startling me out of my stupor. I realized I'd been standing motionless for a good five minutes waiting for the coffee.

"Who's there?" I called. The kitchen is right off the entryway of the house. The house that seems so much emptier after Janine left. After twenty-three damn good years! At least I *thought* they were good.

"Sergeant Comrow." His voice was way too energetic for the time of day. He must have had a good night's sleep. I envied him that much, at least.

"What?" Why the hell would a sergeant be on my porch?

When I opened the door the sight startled me. There, in full red-white-and-blue glory, all of five feet tall and maybe a hundred pounds, looking every bit of eighty years old, stood Uncle Sam.

Yep. That one. The guy from those old recruiting posters, who's always looking right at the camera and pointing his finger in that menacing way.

"Oh, shit," I said, before I could stop myself.

"Don't swear, son. It's not becoming of a representative of the world's most respected nation."

The old man took off his top hat, the white one with the blue band and sparkly star in the middle, revealing a full head of hair just as white as his billy-goat beard. He brushed past me on his way into my kitchen and rummaged around in the cabinets.

"Got any Earl Grey?" he asked, grunting slightly as he stood on tiptoe.

"Uh, no," I said. "I just made some coffee. Would you ..." I paused, and ran my hand over my eyes. *Am I hallucinating?* "Would you like a cup?"

"Pshaw," he waved a hand at me dismissively. "Never touch the stuff. Stunts your growth."

At that I laughed, because coming from him, as if *that* was his non-stunted form, was just a bit too much.

Uncle Sam stopped his exploration of my spice rack and turned to me, striding with purpose the three steps across my kitchen. "Listen, son," he said, pointing that finger. "I'm serious. And you better shape up that attitude of yours or Basic's gonna eat you up and spit you out under a week." He paused, staring directly into my eyes from ten inches lower, and making me feel like a lily wilting under 100-degree Arizona sunshine.

"Okay, mister," I said, backing up. "My apologies." That seemed to work, as he turned on a heel and headed for my refrigerator.

"What's the problem then?" he asked. "Why are you late for registration?"

I shook my head. "I don't know what you're talking about, sir." I did *not* want that bony index finger turned my way.

"Oh yes you do," came the muffled reply from inside my refrigerator. "You're on the list for reporting to Camp Marquette, as of oh eight hundred hours two days ago. You aren't there, now, because you're here. I've been sent to retrieve you."

His pointed chin came back out, wrapped around the leftover fried chicken from two nights ago. Janine brought it home, just before she left; man, I wish we could sit down and just talk.

"I still don't understand," I said. "I'm not supposed to be in basic training. I've never heard of Camp Marquette. And I've never even *thought* of joining the armed forces."

At that, my refrigerator tinkled as it closed, the tartar sauce banging against the Tropicana.

"Look, son," Uncle Sam said, leaning a bony shoulder against the handle, and launching into what seemed like a well-rehearsed speech. "I don't know all your ins and outs, why you're running away. Some are trying to get away from their father, or their mother, or both. Some get a girl in trouble and need to take care of her. Some just know they need a little discipline. Some, they think we're still fighting the Japs, they think they'll get to shoot some yellow fellas, become a hero."

He sighed, put his arms folded across his chest, and looked at me. From this distance, I could see he too was really, truly tired, despite the bravado. "Doesn't matter what your story is, I've heard them all. Point is, you signed up to join the United States Army, and I'm here to help you fulfill your end of the bargain. The Army is not easy. But it also does not take broken promises lightly. Now, you may feel that it's not right for you after a week of PT and KP and LP. But that's for a week away. Right now, we got to get you in the truck. You packed?" He came to my shoulder and put a hand on it, tried to turn me. Maybe to head to my room?

"Sir, I still don't know what you're trying to pull. I have no idea why you think I signed up to the Army, but I can assure you, I did not."

"Peterson," he said, "let's go. I'm tired of your bull spit. I got five more pickups today, and if we don't get a move on, I'll miss dinner."

And there it was. "Oh, sorry, simple mistake, I'm not named Peterson. I'm Harrison, actually. Harrison Carver. You must have the wrong house."

That stopped him. Uncle Sam stepped back a moment, pulled out a paper from his pocket, unfolded it. "This is 425 Cherry Street?"

"Yes, sir."

"In Springfield, Minnesota?"

"Yes, sir."

He scrunched his eyebrows.

"But you're not Lance Peterson?"

"No, sir."

"Does he live here?"

I shook my head. "Not unless he's a ghost. I've been here for ten years. And I bought this place from my parents who lived here thirty years before that."

Uncle Sam scratched his beard, then alternated between that and patting down his pockets for something else.

"Carver?" he said, looking at me.

I nodded. *Mmm, hmm.*

"Springfield?" Again I nodded.

"425 Cherry Street?" I grabbed my wallet from the counter and opened it up, taking out my driver's license. I held it out to him.

He spent a minute looking back and forth between me and the picture on my license. He even stepped to the front door, red-and-white stripey pants swishing with the effort, red sequined shoes tap-tap-tapping, to open my door, find the numbers attached to the frame, and cross-reference them with my driver's license and his paper. He stopped and stood stock still for a good ten seconds.

But then he turned to me, wide-eyed, and with a voice that trembled. "Carver," he said, "What's this on your driver's license?" He pointed with a suddenly trembling finger to the issue date.

"Oh," I said, "That's when I got the license about, um, seven months ago?" I did a little mental math. "Nine, actually."

Uncle Sam turned white as his beard. "Carver," he said, "Why does that say two-zero-one-six?"

"Because it was issued in June of two thousand sixteen, about nine months ago now." I held out my hand and took back my license. "Why?"

Uncle Sam held frame for another few seconds, gears turning. Then, slowly, he held out his paper to me. It was covered with that old-time manual typewriter kind of letters. I thought that was a nice touch. The Army must be harkening back to better days, with some pomp and show. Maybe it helped to ease some fears.

I glanced through it. Indeed, it was a letter reminding Mister Peterson that he did commit to two years of service to the United States Army, that he was expected to show up at Camp Marquette in good physical condition (I glanced at my dad-bod, and wondered how Uncle Sam could have made that mistake), and that he was expected at 0800 hours on Tuesday, March 13, 1956.

Wait ... today was Saturday, March 18. But not anywhere close to 1956.

Whoa. I think I figured out Uncle Sam's problem.

•　　　•　　　•

Uncle Sam was over sixty years out of time. I had no clue what that meant. My mind immediately went to time travel, but then I remembered a movie line — if time travel ever existed, then it has always existed, so we should have seen evidence of it already. Therefore, since we see no evidence of it, it must not exist.

But —

I'm pretty sure Uncle Sam, the short, aggressive old man on my linoleum with orders to get a batch of recruits off to Camp Marquette would disagree. He still thought it was 1956, a fact made very clear over the next few hours as we chatted about the war he thought he was recruiting for (Korea) and things that had happened since then (Vietnam, trickle-down economics, and blowjobs in the

White House). I mean, can you blame him? Suppose *you* wake up fifty years in the future. How would you react to all new technologies, and a world which knows so much more than you do?

I showed him cable television. I showed him the Internet. I showed him porn. He didn't like that too much.

He showed me his list of collections. Not only was he to get Lance Peterson, right here on Spring Street, he had two others in the next town over who hadn't shown up, and three from a smallish place about sixty miles the other direction.

But, what to do? None of it made sense. We sat in my kitchen, at 10:30 am, cradling my cold Natty Light and his lukewarm milk with chocolate powder. Uncle Sam didn't really have an answer, and neither did I. It didn't do much good to try and figure out the physics of the situation, since neither of us was remotely experienced with math or science backgrounds. My Google, Bing, and dark web searches turned up nothing, as I rather expected them to. Why should they? Either time travel was impossible and Sam was a great actor, or I was an unsuspecting trailblazer. If so, I suddenly had a lot of responsibility. I might have to make sure the rest of the world knew what was possible.

Could I do it? Did I have the public relations abilities to get that done? Who knew. All I could tell was I may be —

"Wait," said Sam. He'd been reading Wikipedia when I turned introspective. "Carver, come look at this."

He was on the page to something called a "Multiverse" theory.

Apparently, there are people who believe this whacked-out idea that every time there's a decision in the universe, it splits into two (or more) paths, with one representing each individual decision. Everything's possible, always and forever. I immediately saw that it was bullshit, and said so.

Sam didn't rebuke me this time. I couldn't tell if it was desensitization due to being in 2017 for all of four hours, or perhaps he'd decided to give up on reforming me. Either way, he let that one slide.

I pointed out the physical impossibility of infinite options, due to the infinite energy required to make that happen. Surprised myself a little with that leap of knowledge.

But it didn't faze him. He kept digging deeper into the subject, so I eventually left and went down to the corner store to refill my stock of Natty Light. I picked up a sixer of YooHoo for Sam, too.

By the time I returned he'd found one of my notebooks and a pen. He'd been scribbling, covering half a dozen sheets with tiny, barely readable scrawl.

"Carver," he said, "I know what we need to do."

There is no "we" here, I thought. This dude is way off his rocker. No way I'm gonna follow him. But I humored the guy. "What's that?"

"We need to finish my mission."

•　　　•　　　•

Despite my skepticism, what Uncle Sam spouted over the next couple of hours actually started making some sense. I couldn't follow it all, 'cause he had some notion about more than the three dimensions of space, and multiple universes, that I thought we'd already got rid of. But something about splitting then recombining later actually made sense.

He figured that if we had split the universe back in the 1950s, when he was still in his original time frame, and he'd made some kind of leap across some extra dimension to this point, then the way for him to get back would be to finish what he had started (this mission of collecting six AWOLs who never showed up for Basic Training), and then that would somehow collapse all these holes in the pants of space-time or something.

I didn't know all the details, and I never really got a clear answer of *why* the world would be that way, but, anyway, about two hours later I found myself driving a 1950s-era Jeep down Highway 72, toward Kipford, where half of his list lived.

The action energized Sam. His eyes sparkled, and his fingers tapped the glass in the window as we drove. He chattered on aimlessly, telling me about the boys he'd recruited over the year, about how his own drill sergeant had had a bad case of night sweats and was real embarrassed about it, about how he'd looked forward to his sister's liver-and-onions every time he got leave to go over to her place for Sunday dinner.

Uncle Sam wasn't a bad guy, I decided about half an hour into the trip. I could see myself liking him. He was like that sort-of-friendly but a little-bit-stand-offish old bachelor down the street that you want to know, but don't want to spend a lot of time with.

We reached Kipford about three in the afternoon. Sam had pulled another set of papers out of his pocket, that all looked like the one he'd been holding on my porch. Once he had an address, I let GPS take over. Sam marveled. Much of modern life was amazing, and the rest was overwhelming. I couldn't disagree.

When we pulled up on the house, I waited in the driver's seat. Sam strode purposefully to the front door and pushed the doorbell. In a moment, a seventy-something woman answered, dressed in jeans, a chambray shirt, and gardening gloves. They chatted for a moment, and then she disappeared. Laughing, it looked like.

In another minute a similarly-aged gentleman appeared at the door. He looked Sam up and down, then began to chuckle. Sam then began a heated exchange of words. Over the course of about ten minutes, I watched the man go from incredulous to disbelieving to resolute to accepting, all while Sam remained firm, polite, and on-topic. Sam stood still, looked the other in the eye, and did not back down. The other avoided eye contact, gestured wildly, and turned around in circles, running his hands over his bald head a few times.

Finally, the man's shoulders slumped, his arms dropped, and Sam's back straightened. He replaced his hat, and then turned to indicate the Jeep. The old man poked his head inside the house for moment and shouted something, then the two of them strode my way.

They piled into the Jeep's wide front seat with me. I quickly looked around and saw that we wouldn't have space for four more in the back. We were shoulder-to-shoulder up here, and that was that.

"Um, hello," I said, extending a hand to the new guy. "I'm Harrison."

"Henry," he said, with a limp shake. He smelled of woodshop and smoke. I suspected he'd been pursuing his hobby. He leaned in for a whisper. *"What the hell is this?"*

I shook my head and shrugged. *Damned if I know.* We both straightened as Sam took out another paper and gave us the next address. His look of satisfaction, a huge smile that reached all the way to his eyes, propelled us forward.

•   •   •

Henry and I jounced and bounced together as the Jeep rumbled down the street. This little town of Kipford looked like it had seen better days.

Back when Sam had been first on the job, it was probably a happy, bustling community. Families lived here, they worked at the bank and the school and the factory, they sent their sons to the Army or to college in Minneapolis, they went to church on Sunday. But this was clearly one of the places stuck in time – an aging population, little growth, little impulse to even *try*.

Why? Most of what might get started here was already being done in ten or fifteen other small towns around the county, and probably better too, because they were already decades ahead. What hope did a place like this have to survive?

We drove slowly, turning down this street or that one, past small two-bedroom houses and occasional parks, old store fronts which had faded and cracked signs still advertising wedding dresses, or pet grooming, or "Good Eats, Great Friends". I wondered whether everyone was in on the collective delusion that they might still make it, or if some people were just too simple, too ignorant, too caught up in the nostalgia of the past to care.

Despite all that Sam was quite animated. As we drove he told us stories of Kipford, relating to all the places we passed. His cousin lived here, so he'd spent many Saturday nights as a youth hanging out and badgering neighborhood dogs. He spoke reverently of a time, a hundred years gone now, that seemed to be not so backwards as I always had assumed about the past.

Maybe there was something special about that time. Maybe that's why he remembered it so strongly. Maybe that's why he was pulled out of that time, across the intervening years of decline and decay to *this point*, when he could skip the heartbreak and pain of watching something so beloved fall to the ravages of time.

Wish I could have skipped that part.

Sam stopped talking abruptly, in the middle of the story about kissing a pretty girl back behind her shed, which we were apparently passing that same shed, and leaned forward. "There!" He said, and pointed forcefully. "Six-one-five-two."

We pulled into the driveway, and Sam hopped out to repeat his performance with Henry. Similar things happened. The door opened on its own but this time it was a middle-aged man, probably the AWOL recruit's son, or perhaps grandson.

After a shout inside the house an old man, pot-bellied and, like Henry, balding, appeared on the porch. I couldn't tell what they were saying, but I could see that Number Three wasn't having any part of it. He wanted to go back inside. Sam stopped him at least twice with a hand on his arm, which Three shook off like an enraged bear.

He tried to get back inside his door, and then the strangest thing happened. Sam, with a quiet flick of his wrist, waved a couple of fingers. Instantly the other changed. Instead of defiant, proud, and belligerent, he showed a calm, relaxed, and willing posture. He stopped struggling and looked Sam in the eye. Together they turned and walked towards the Jeep. Henry and I shared a look, that wide-eyed, disbelieving look that said, "What did I just see?" I couldn't explain it, and neither could Henry. *Did he do that to us, too?* Sam squished in front and Leroy Jackson dumped himself into the backseat.

•   •   •

Henry and I glanced at each other a few times as we kept driving. Uncle Sam had his new paper out, and chattered excitedly as we moved on. He introduced us around and we shook hands with Leroy, who didn't say anything, shell-shocked.

For my part, I still couldn't believe that there were actually two people that Sam had found, and that they were still alive, still in the same town 60 years later, and that not only were they there, they'd agreed to play along with Sam's idea. I didn't quite understand it all, but in between the directions, the reflections of Kipford that came out as we passed the remnants of history, he interspersed enough details of his theory to keep us believing.

It had something to do with waveforms and supersymmetry. Apparently, and this is all I understand about it, because I have no clue how he actually came up with this theory, there had not only been a split in our universe long ago, there would be some kind of reconciliation that would take place when Sam's mission was finished. I never got the gist of why he hadn't been able to do what he was supposed to back in 1956, but it sounded like a family emergency had kept him from performing his collection as usual, on the day after everyone was supposed to show up. So he waited a day, and woke up the next. Drove over to my house and somehow found himself sixty-one years out of time.

I was pretty skeptical of the plan. Yet Sam's enthusiasm was infections. I could see why the Army had used him for recruitment, back when patriotism was so high despite the real dangers of the outside world. People still love their country today, but I suspect that the low support for the Army comes from the feeling that the threats are much less significant than they used to be.

We picked up Paul Zink with only a little delay. He hadn't been there right when we arrived, so his wife invited Sam in for tea. He called back to see if we wanted any, and I thought about it, but the idea of being inside Mrs. Zink's kitchen just seemed one step too far for me.

Zink himself pulled up in a dusty, red pickup truck half an hour after we arrived. He'd been on an errand run, so he had to change his shirt before he came with us. He sat in the backseat and talked friendly.

Apparently, Paul had been wondering when this day might come. He remembered missing his appointment for Boot Camp and expecting them to come looking for him. Maybe Henry and Leroy had, too, and that's why they came so willingly. Maybe they figured they'd gotten six decades worth of reprieve, so they didn't have any kind of argument. But when I looked at the men in the Jeep with us, I couldn't imagine any of them passing even the most basic physical exam.

Was that part of their calculation, too? Prove they weren't in shape, and flunk out? Or did they actually believe Uncle Sam, and that they were going to go defend their mother Country from those *any and all* threats which came at her?

Clearly, they had some curiosity, too. Well, maybe not Leroy. He didn't have much of anything, just sat in the back seat next to Paul and said nothing. Everyone else was quite jolly, and then we were back in Springfield half an hour after sundown.

Uncle Sam and I began an argument about the next step. He wanted to push forward and find the last two guys on his list. I wanted to get these other guys a hotel room for the night. Sam wasn't having that because they might run again if left unsupervised.

In the end, we compromised, which meant everyone got less than they wanted. We would stay at my house and the boys would sleep on couches in the basement. We'd head out for the other two early in the morning. But only if Sam agreed that we would actually leave early in the morning, so that if Janine did decide to come back before church, she wouldn't think hobos had overtaken me.

•　　•　　•

Paul snored. Henry & Leroy were out like a light. Sam got up three times to pee. Me, I just kind of kept watch over these new, strange men in my basement. Despite the lack of sleep before, I'd been jazzed up all day. I didn't want to admit it, but this was kind of fun. At least I'd have a story to tell, and maybe that would be enough to convince Janine that I wasn't so boring after all.

I snoozed a little bit, but having so many people in my rec room wasn't really comfortable to me, so I got up early. Starting at a little past four I did some of my own Internet research on strange things like time warps and black holes. I never did get the certainty that

Sam had. Maybe I should have gone past the first page of Google, but, hey, that's not our style these days, is it?

Everyone else started stirring about six and I made a pot of coffee, which we all drank, except for Sam. Nobody talked much. I guessed it was the weirdness of standing around in some stranger's kitchen in yesterday's clothes that kind of mutes the conversation. I made a few piles of toast, and found some bacon to fry up for breakfast, but nobody really ate, again except Sam. He was ready and raring to go, so about seven thirty we found ourselves scrunched back into the Jeep.

"Over to Bryant Place," Sam said. I knew the area, so it was my turn to create some commentary.

"That's where my sister Kathleen used to live," I said, as we passed a two-story with a white fence out front. Springfield was in better shape than Kipford, but even now you could see that the edges were fraying. Another few years, and maybe even this place would start to crumble. The one main business in town, that made all kinds of brushes and brooms, had been going strong for all of eighty years, but even that was in danger from offshore production and the redirection of manual labor.

As my ramblings continued, I noticed the men in the car with me had fallen silent. Maybe they were reflecting on the same sort of general, slow, inevitable decline that they, too, could see coming. They wanted so badly to reverse it — to make things go back to the way they *used* to be – that their desires seemed to float out of them and hang in the air like a tangible, visible fog. Or an aura. As we pulled up to the destination Sam spoke.

"Boys," he said, and I noticed a hitch in his voice. "I thank you for coming on this mission with me." He turned to each one in turn, and saluted. Each simply stared, mystified.

"I know it's weird," he continued. "And maybe I'm just a crazy old man. Believe you me, I'm wondering just what I'm doing here myself a time or two these past two days."

He opened the door and popped out, then looked back at me. "But," he said, with a leprechaun's twinkle in his eye, "I *guarantee* you'll never have something like this again! I *feel* it. This just feels right — like music in my soul. This is what I'm *supposed* to do." He shut the door, turned to the walkway, and headed up.

This experience turned out to be different, though. Instead of a brief conversation on the porch, Sam had barely pushed the button when the door opened. An old man opened it up wearing only boxer shorts and carrying a shotgun. He leveled the gun at Sam's chest, and instinctively Sam threw up his hands and backed away. He walked slowly in the same way until he bumped his backside into the car door. He opened and got in, never breaking eye contact with the deranged, derelict old man staring down the sights.

Once inside, Sam calmly tore up the paper, and tossed it out the window to flutter down to the driveway.

"Carver," he said calmly, "Driver to Pierson Place, please." I did, and it was about a minute down the road that any of us let out the collective breath we had been holding.

•   •   •

So that was it. We were down to our last name on Sam's list. He'd started with six to find and return to

Camp Marquette. I was the replacement for one who'd probably moved away fifty years ago and never looked back. Henry, Leroy, and Paul we'd found. I asked about the guy with the shotgun, and Sam simply said, "Looks like William couldn't be bothered today."

We discussed for a moment what that meant. "Don't you have to complete all your objectives?" I asked. "I mean, isn't that essentially why we're doing this?"

Sam shook his head. His little white beard trailed his chin as it moved back and forth like a pendulum, or a hypnotist's watch, mesmerizing the audience.

"No," he replied, finally. "Our COs give us the general path, and they let us figure out how to make it happen. If we relied on them for every decision, we'd never get anywhere. They'd be overwhelmed with trying to give too much detail, we'd wait too long, and the opportunity would be lost."

Paul spoke up from the back seat. "C-O?"

"Commanding Officer," Sam replied. I knew that term from television and movies. I was surprised Paul had to ask. Maybe he'd been inside his house so long that he hadn't spent much time with the outside world.

"But what happens when you don't have six men with you?" I asked. "Would that mean you're not yet finished?"

"Well," said Sam, "seeing as how I'm not entirely sure how this is gonna go, I'm doing my best and improvising a little bit. It's like when the CO tells you to 'take that hill'. He doesn't say, 'Bring fifteen men to the south side, then advance thirty paces, spreading out like thieves in the night.' You know what I mean? My CO gave me a set of papers. If I return with 4 men and 4 papers, who's to know the difference?"

Henry shook his head. His voice, when he spoke, had a much lighter quality than expected, given his heavy cheeks and oversized belly. "But, why do it at all? Why not just rip up all your letters when you first met Harrison over there?" He cocked a hitchhiker's thumb at me. I drove on and pulled in to Pierson Place. We still had one more stop, and I hoped for a sort of resolution to the whole thing.

Sam sat for just a moment before answering. "Conscience," he finally said. "I could, in no good conscience, completely abandon my responsibilities. I have to, for my own mind and clean spirit, believe I've done what I can to finish what I've started.

"No, I didn't find Lance over at Harrison Carver's house. But I looked for him. I can mark him AWOL on the form and feel good about it. You three," and he looked in turn to the gentlemen from Kipford. "You're all here, because you felt the calling. You know what it means to keep your promises.

"This last one," he waved an arm back over his shoulder, "that last one was some nut job, definitely. The Army cannot take nut jobs, so I made an executive decision to reject his application. Both sides are better off without him.

"And now we come here. Outside Arthur Fratelli's place." Sam looked at the brown-and-white wood-sided home, with a falling-down bench set among a dozen front yard gnomes of various sporting poses. "Fratelli. Good Italian name. My grandmother came from Venice with her parents when she was just a few years old." Sam looked like he was about to cry. "Good woman, she was. Such a good woman." He paused, just a moment, then collected himself and stepped out of the car. "Wait here, boys," he said.

We could have done no different.

It was at least two minutes Sam stood on the porch before anyone answered. He, as before, stood hat in hand to talk to a slim, stooped woman who answered the door. We waited in silence, staring through the windshield at a scene we'd all been on the other side of.

It was strange, thinking about Sam's journey, and about mine. Was there something special about me that it was my door he knocked on first? Was it a consequence of having bought the house years before, never really knowing the town or the history, and yet here I was, an integral part of whatever quantum-mechanics mumbo-jumbo that was going on?

Paul and Leroy were amiably chatting in the back seat; they were speculating about what might happen when we got to Camp Marquette. Neither understood any more about Sam's plan than I did, even though he'd spent a good hour the night before talking about it. Each time he mentioned a waveform, all I could see in my head was Hawaii, and the black sand beach my wife and I had vacationed on a few years earlier, and the bluest of waves breaking on the shore, and I would get so distracted by the image and the yearning memory that I would stop concentrating on Sam and his plan, so it would take me a few moments to catch up. Something he said kind of bothered me, though I never really knew how to put it into words. It had something to do with waves canceling each other out, but I didn't have a good enough grasp of the real physics of the situation to even *think* about the metaphysics.

So we waited. Sam talked with the old woman, and then she stepped aside to let him into her home. He went willingly, without so much as a glance back at us. Together in the car, we made eye contact, raised eyebrows, made little "humph" noises.

I turned on the radio.

Paul spat out the window.

Henry farted.

The front door opened once more, and Sam reappeared. He was carrying a big metal football.

"Oh, god," said Leroy.

"Oh, no," I said. I shook my head. "You've got to be kidding me."

Sam wore a somber expression – eyes turned down, mouth set in a stiff line. He stopped just before getting in the car, held the urn with one hand, and saluted Fratelli's widow with the other. She straightened on the porch and returned the salute. Then he opened the backseat car door and strapped the urn into the middle belt.

He got in the front seat, turned to me, and said, "Camp Marquette, Son. It's about a two-hour drive. You're gonna want to get gas at exit six, about twenty minutes up the road." He stared straight ahead, said nothing else.

I shifted it into drive.

•   •   •

After exit six, we rode most of the last ninety minutes in silence, only broken by the occasional burp or unintentional cough. I even kept the radio off. Something just didn't feel right trying to make a fun situation with the ashes of a dead man in the back seat.

At least we weren't quite so crowded. In the copilot position, Sam stared straight ahead. His nervous, anticipatory energy from the day before had disappeared. Now he was a ball of calm. I suspected it was an act.

We drove onto the base about half past eleven on a Sunday morning. I don't know just what their schedule is, but out in the real world, Monday to Friday is work, Saturday is play, Sunday is church. If you're out on the roads, it's cause you're going to Hell, and you're probably ashamed of that, so everyone is quiet, keeps to themselves, and just goes about their business.

I suspected the same might be true for the military base, a ninety-acre compound carved out of the Minnesota old-growth forest. This place had been smoothed by the glaciers when the white man arrived, and we'd barely made a dent since. All the buildings were square, flat, dark grey, and a single story, like they too were afraid to stand out against the backdrop.

We stopped at a guard house, where once again Sam went to work. The two twenty-something guards wanted ID, they wanted a purpose, they wanted a destination. Sam said something to one; asked him about a grandfather. That instantly brightened the young man's face, and he stepped back. Not to let us in, but it at least opened the conversation. Sam took the opportunity to point to the Jeep, to the urn in the backseat, to say something about a quick memorial for a long-time veteran. Apparently Uncle Sam is not above verbal manipulation to supplement his hypnotism.

But still, no dice. The one young man seemed ready to let us pass, but the other held fast his position. No paper, no entry, was his motto, and he was damn sure he wasn't going to get reprimanded over something like this.

I wished I knew how to help. Maybe Sam could do that little finger-wag. And maybe he would have, but he didn't want one of them to see him doing it to the other one.

"Hey Sam," I called. He turned to catch my eye. "Why don't you go talk to our friend a little more closely," and I nodded in Frowny's direction. "I've got a question."

I stepped out and got the attention of Smiley. He was a young thing, big ears still sticking out from his hat, broad shoulders, face with pimples and plenty of scars from them as well. His demeanor, while remaining pleasant, became more guarded. He was suspicious. *For good reason,* I thought. *Hell, even I don't know what we're doing here.*

I asked the little guy a few questions about his background. He'd come from a small family, small town, small body, all combined to make him feel small, inadequate. So he'd joined the Army to find something larger than himself. And he had such great respect for our mission, he said. He was pretty sure we weren't supposed to be there, but he looked at us and knew we couldn't do any harm.

His name was Pearson. But he went by Specs form the guys in the troop. I told him my nickname was Fuzzy, and I hated it.

"Why, Fuzzy?" he said.

"Because that's all the hair my balls ever grew, just a little peach fuzz," I said, and that made him laugh harder than if George Carlin had walked through the door. I took the moment of his distraction to glance over at Sam. He wasn't finished yet. The other guy was still adamant that we weren't going to get by. Pearson and I chatted for another two minutes, then I could see Sam start to get mad. His voice, too, got louder, and it looked as if he somehow got taller.

I excused myself from Pearson and went to join their conversation. I asked Sam to back off; then, I talked quietly to the other gentleman. Soldier. I had to remind myself of that.

"Sir, may I ask your name?"

"Private Backus," was the terse reply.

"Good afternoon, Soldier Backus. I am not a soldier. I'm simply a civilian."

"I understand, but it looks like your grandfather here does not. This is a restricted area. Nobody gets on the base without permission."

I thought hard. Did I have the guts to lie to a man with a gun, in a situation where, if I survived, I might even end up in jail? Hell, I needed *something* to liven up my life, and if this wasn't proof enough to Janine, I couldn't imagine out what would be.

"Well," I began, "I'm not supposed to say this, because it's a surprise for your immediate superior."

"What does Lieutenant George have to do with this?"

"Well, you see, the remains that we have with us in the backseat today are actually those of Lieutenant George's uncle. I'm another one of those uncles. My brother died about two weeks ago and Lieutenant George was unavoidably detained on the base here. I promised him that we, my other family members and I ..." I swept my arm towards the gentlemen staring at us with wide eyes.

My heart thumped so hard it felt like my head was pulsating. "We've come to allow Lieutenant George to pay his respects. I'm sorry that nobody called to let you know we were coming. We couldn't really tell him, or we would ruin the surprise."

Backus looked at me for a good thirty seconds without moving. Didn't breathe, didn't blink, didn't lick his lips or anything. I tried to hold frame as much as possible, but I felt myself shifting my weight from foot to foot. *Please believe me, please believe me.*

Finally Backus spoke, his voice no softer, his eyes no less penetrating. "Yeah, that sounds like a pretty shitty thing to do. Would be right up the base commander's alley not to let someone go to his uncle's funeral."

He stepped back and nodded at Pearson. I don't think he really believed me, but I think he *wanted* to believe me. Which was probably the same thing. My heart filled my chest with two hundred beats a minute of pure power, and I had to steady myself so I didn't fall over from the shock. But I'd done it. Pearson pushed a button that started the gate swinging open. We were through.

•　　•　　•

Back in the car, Sam stared at me for just a moment. "Carver," he said, "What in tarnation was that?"

I shrugged. "Improvisation," I said, and gripped the wheel. "Thinking on my feet. Thought you knew a thing or two about that."

He just snuffed a breath out through his nostrils and gave me a sly grin. "Forward, then!"

We followed Sam's pointed directions to get to a recruiter's office. I had no clue how he could tell which one it was. All the buildings and all the streets looked identical to me. There weren't even any numbers on them.

We pulled up to another one of those "same as everything else" and tumbled out. The stiff ankles and hips of Paul, Henry, and Leroy forced them into limps for the first dozen steps or so, until their blood had coursed through their veins long enough that it had washed off the internal rust.

We all walked, hobbled, or stumbled inside, Sam holding the urn cradled in the crook of his arm. He'd given me the stack of papers.

Sam marched us through the door directly into some kind of high-ranking official's office. There were photographs on three of the walls that looked like recruiting classes. There was a brown, wide, low desk with very few papers on it and a name plate that said MAJOR KILLIAN. The filing cabinet in the corner was stuffed, I assumed, with all of the things that would have been on that desk in any other professional office.

We waited just a minute, then heard a door open. "What the hell is this?" came a loud, high-pitched voice. A female voice. And in a few seconds, a woman — stocky, taller than Sam at five-seven or so, with a tight braid to her long brown hair — marched inside.

"I want to know who the hell you think you are, mister, and why my front gate is pulling me away from my Sunday morning fuck just to see your sorry asses?" She stomped around the room, staring at each one of us in turn. By the time she got to Sam, all the rest had already withered under her gaze.

Sam spoke first. He appeared unbowed. Being back on the military base, finally interacting with a superior officer again after spending so much time out in the field must have done something for him. Instead of acting subservient, like a whipped dog, he stood up straight, shoulders back, head high. He saluted her, and held it for the two seconds it took her to respond in kind.

Then he took of his hat, and spoke in a regular, stiff manner. "Sergeant Samuel Comrow, reporting for duty, ma'am. Responding to my instructions, I have retrieved as many of the unreported recruits as were available to find." He waved a hand, and I figured that was my cue. I handed over the stack of papers. She took them without looking at me and started riffling through them while Sam continued.

"Recruit Lance Peterson missing in action. Supposed AWOL and out of the country. Recruit Henry Black reporting for duty," and he pointed to Henry, who stood up straighter at the mention of his name, his big belly still sagging over his belt and his shoes untied.

"Recruit Leroy Jackson reporting for duty," and Leroy did the same, pushing his glasses up from the end of his nose. Sam introduced Paul, and then all three saluted. They held their pose. The major did not return their salutes. She waited for Sam to finish, an exasperated look on her face.

"Recruit Arthur Fratelli," Sam said, and presented the urn. "DOA." He set the urn on her desk, and backed away.

The three men hadn't moved in ten seconds or so. I imagined they were getting tired of holding that pose. Sam joined them in salute, and I, feeling all kinds of extra, took two steps backwards.

Major Killian took a deep breath. She said, "At ease," and then the others relaxed. When she spoke next, her voice had softened. We knew her place, and ours, so we didn't have to poke and prod any longer. And she didn't have to maintain that high intensity.

"Gentlemen," she said, speaking to the three recruits. "I don't know what this guy told you, but, frankly, you're not in the Army." She tore the papers in half, then in half again, and dropped them in the waste basket.

"And you," she said, turning to Sam. "That's a pretty nice outfit. Where'd you get that, Party City? I bet you'd be a hit at the Independence Day Parade. Want to come back next year?" Sam sputtered and coughed, evidently unnerved.

"I'm sorry, what?"

Major Killian shook her head. "Listen," she said, "I don't know what this stunt was, if Corporal Johnston put you up to this or what, but, well done. You managed to talk your way onto a restricted military base without proper authorization. You all look harmless enough, so I'm not going to press charges on anyone. My gate guards, however, will be spending the afternoon doing pushups till I puke."

She began indicating with her arms that we should go. I made a quick detour before heading for the door. She herded us out and back into the Jeep. Sam, urn in hand, got back into the front seat.

Killian opened her door. "You gentlemen need to leave. I can't have you here. I'll follow to make sure you don't get lost."

Sam's voice was soft, disbelieving. "Harrison, what went wrong?"

"I don't know," I said. But I did. I knew.

Sam was out of time. Out of place. He was maybe even out of his mind, and whether or not the suit and the hair and those papers had *looked* convincing enough to make me and four other naïve old farts believe him, the major knew her shit. She didn't want to spend any more time with us explaining all our mistakes and problems, so she simply dismissed us, sent us back the way we came.

"I guess," I said, as the Jeep rumbled along the flat asphalt, "that she didn't see it the same way you did."

• • •

The drive back was quiet, uneventful. We first went to Kipford, and returned Paul, and Henry, and Leroy. Their wives greeted them at their doors with appropriate belittlement for having been gone all day, neglecting to call, ignoring their text messages. Personally, I kind of liked the idea that they'd had a day away for a guys' adventure. Some bonding, something that was a break from the norm, and I could see why they would have wanted to hold onto that little fantasy of *maybe* a little while longer.

We returned to Bryant Place and dropped off Fratelli's urn with his widow, then headed back to my house. I couldn't understand exactly how this was going to go, but I hoped that Sam would get his resolution, or his waveform collapse, or whatever he hoped would happen. I also hoped that Janine would be there so that she could watch him fade into the background with me.

We pulled in to my house around sunset. I'd been gone all day, and most of the day before. I was tired, stiff from the ride, and confused as all get-out. But I felt a smile on my face, despite Sam's confused eyes and slumped shoulders, and the fact that Janine's blue sedan was not in the driveway. He walked me to the porch.

I stuck out a hand to shake. He refused, then stepped back and saluted me one final time. I responded in kind, then watched him take the keys and get behind the wheel. He could barely see over it, and I wondered how he could even reach the pedals.

I would have liked to have had more conversation about the day, but he had left so abruptly, and so silently, that asking him to wait around to satisfy my curiosity didn't seem right. He backed out of the drive, hit the gas, and high-tailed it down along Route 9 and over the hill into oblivion.

I never saw Sam again, but every once in a while I'll get a letter or an e-mail from Paul or Henry. I don't know how they found me, and it's not very interesting to read their updates, but each time, I stop and wonder.

How did Sam get on my porch in the first place? And was he telling the truth? Would he have actually returned to his own timeline if he'd convinced the major and enlisted those recruits? Maybe when he drove away, he and his Jeep scampered back through a time warp and he ended up back in 1956. Or was there perhaps one of those other worlds in which that *did* happen, and over there is a different Harrison Carver sitting on his porch wondering what might have happened if *his* Killian hadn't been so open? Did they all transform in front of his eyes to be sixty-years-younger versions of themselves, skinny and with full heads of hair and no liver spots and perfect eyesight, and walked straight out the door, to their uniform fitting? Did they watch their version of me disappear, blending into the background while Sam and the boys and the major kept on going?

It's too much to think about. But occasionally, I'll pull out some six sheets of hand-written notes and four or five taped-together old-time typewriter pages salvaged from the wastebasket in Killian's office, my only mementos of that weekend. I'll grab a beer, sit on the back porch, have a little cry about what's not around any longer, and consider the possibilities.

ABOUT THE AUTHOR

Stephan James lives in Missouri with several children, several pets, and several works in progress. He fiction has been published in *The Arcanist* and *Fall Into Fantasy 2022*, while his non-fiction (as Stephan Mathys) has been published at *Story Unlikely* and *Wabash Magazine*. Find more of his work at *stephanjameswrites.com*.

YOU MIGHT ALSO ENJOY

CHOOSE YOUR TRUTH
by Jo Miles

Truth is obsolete.
May the best lies win.

THE CREDO OF COMRADE JANUARY
by Robert Bagnall

Solar explosions known as "The Pulse"
have rendered all electronics useless and
sent Mankind back to a pre-digital age.

DENISOVAN HARMONY
by DJ Cockburn

You're watching the first Homo denisova
to walk the earth in a hundred and fifty
centuries grope their way into adolescence.

Available in digital and trade paperback editions from
Water Dragon Publishing
waterdragonpublishing.com

www.ingramcontent.com/pod-product-compliance
Lightning Source LLC
Chambersburg PA
CBHW021601310726
48972CB00003B/902